GRANBY PUBLIC LIBRARY
3 2539 13859 0772

- HERGÉ -
★

THE ADVENTURES OF TINTIN

RED RACKHAM'S TREASURE

W9-CCV-945

Property of Town of Granby
Granby Public Library - Children's Room
15 North Granby Road
Granby, CT 06035
WITHDRAWN

Little, Brown and Company
New York   Boston

Original Album: *Red Rackham's Treasure*
Renewed Art Copyright © 1945, 1973 by Casterman, Belgium
Text Copyright © 1959 by Egmont UK Limited

Translated by Leslie Lonsdale-Cooper and Michael Turner

Additional Material
Art Copyright © Hergé/Moulinsart 2011
Text Copyright © Moulinsart 2011

www.casterman.com
www.tintin.com

US Edition Copyright © 2011 by Little, Brown and Company, a division of Hachette Book Group, Inc.
Published pursuant to agreement with Editions Casterman and Moulinsart S.A.
Not for sale in the British Commonwealth.
All rights reserved. Except as permitted under the U.S. Copyright Act of 1976,
no part of this publication may be reproduced, distributed, or transmitted in any form or by any means,
or stored in a database or retrieval system, without the prior written permission of the publisher.

Little, Brown and Company
Hachette Book Group
1290 Avenue of the Americas, New York, NY 10104
Visit us at lb-kids.com

The publisher is not responsible for websites (or their content) that are not owned by the publisher.

First Edition: May 2011

The characters and events portrayed in this book are fictitious. Any similarity to real persons,
living or dead, is coincidental and not intended by the author.

ISBN: 978-0-316-13384-5
2011921033
5 4
SC
Printed in China

Tintin and Snowy

Tintin is a brave young reporter
who loves to solve mysteries and fight crime!
Tintin's faithful dog, Snowy,
follows his master wherever he goes.

Captain Haddock

Tintin's best friend. Although quick to anger,
the captain has a heart of gold and would lay down his life
for his young companion.

Professor Calculus

An eccentric scientist who is more than a little hard of hearing.
Professor Calculus makes up for endless misunderstandings
by inventing amazing machines!

Thomson

One half of an accident-prone police team.
You can tell Thomson apart from his colleague by looking
at his mustache: the tips on each side flare out a bit!

Thompson

The other half of a crime-fighting duo that can't stop getting into trouble.
The ends of Thompson's mustache droop downward.

Bill

The talkative chef on board the ship named *Sirius*.
Bill is happy as long as Snowy stays out of his kitchen!

The old shopkeeper

A beady-eyed old man who has a diving suit for sale,
the shopkeeper appears to be able to read Captain Haddock's mind.
Blistering barnacles!

RED RACKHAM'S
TREASURE

* See The Secret of the Unicorn

(1)

Red Rackham's Treasure

THE forthcoming departure of the trawler *Sirius* is arousing speculation in sea-faring circles. Despite the close secrecy which is being maintained, our correspondent understands that the object of the voyage is nothing less than a search for treasure.

This treasure, once the hoard of the pirate Red Rackham, lies in the ship *Unicorn*, sunk at the end of the seventeenth century. Tintin, the famous reporter—whose sensational intervention in the Bird case made headline news—and his friend Captain Haddock, have discovered the exact resting-place of the *Unicorn*,

Mr Tintin? . . .

Yes.

Mr Tintin. I see from this morning's paper that you are going to try and find Red Rackham's treasure. Is that so?

Yes, it is. But . . .

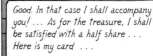

Good. In that case I shall accompany you! . . . As for the treasure, I shall be satisfied with a half share . . . Here is my card . . .

!

Is . . . is that really your name? . . .

So it seems, young man.

Look, Captain . . .

Blistering barnacles!

RED RACKHAM

But, if I'm not mistaken, sir, your name is simply Rackham. 'Red' is just a nickname. In which case I see no connection between you and Red Rackham the pirate . . .

RRRING

Mr Tintin? . . . I demand my share of the treasure! . . . I am Red Rackham's sole descendant! . . .

He's not. I am!

He's not. I am!

It's me!

Don't listen! I'm the one!

I am! And here's my family tree!

Leave this to me! We'll soon see if there's a real Rackham among that crew!

You're all descendants of Red Rackham are you?

Good! Well, I'm descended from Sir Francis Haddock, who killed Red Rackham in single combat . . . and blew up his ship . . . And there are times . . .

. . . when my ancestor's fighting blood begins to boil!

Avast, freshwater pirates!

What's going on up there?

What a stampede!

Like a lot of wild elephants!

A real herd of elephants!

To be precise: a real herd of elephants!

And there are your records, fancy-dress freebooters!

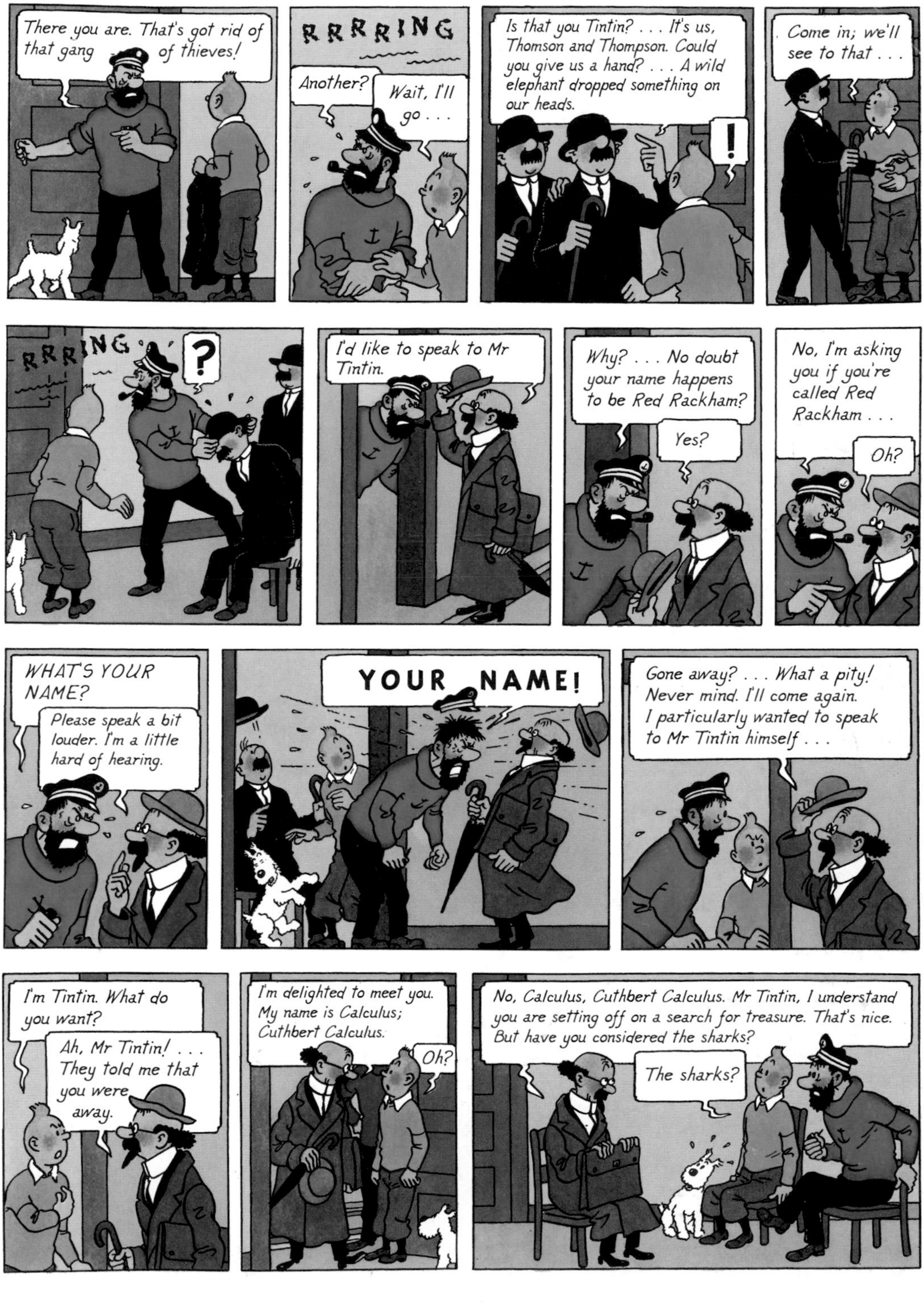
There you are. That's got rid of that gang of thieves!
RRRRING
Another?
Wait, I'll go . . .
Is that you Tintin? . . . It's us, Thomson and Thompson. Could you give us a hand? . . . A wild elephant dropped something on our heads.
!
Come in; we'll see to that . . .
RRRING
?
I'd like to speak to Mr Tintin.
Why? . . . No doubt your name happens to be Red Rackham?
Yes?
No, I'm asking you if you're called Red Rackham . . .
Oh?
WHAT'S YOUR NAME?
Please speak a bit louder. I'm a little hard of hearing.
YOUR NAME!
Gone away? . . . What a pity! Never mind. I'll come again. I particularly wanted to speak to Mr Tintin himself . . .
I'm Tintin. What do you want?
Ah, Mr Tintin! . . . They told me that you were away.
I'm delighted to meet you. My name is Calculus; Cuthbert Calculus.
Oh?
No, Calculus, Cuthbert Calculus. Mr Tintin, I understand you are setting off on a search for treasure. That's nice. But have you considered the sharks?
The sharks?

No, young man, I'm talking about the sharks. I expect you intend to do some diving. In which case, beware of sharks!

But . . .

Don't you agree? . . . But I've invented a machine for underwater exploration, and it's shark-proof. If you'll come to my house with me, I'll show it to you.

I'm very sorry but . . .

No, it's not far. Less than ten minutes . . .

I'm afraid I'm very busy and I . . .

Why of course. Certainly these gentlemen may come too.

It's no good. There's no time! NO TIME!

Good, that's settled. We'll go at once.

I'm so glad you agreed to come!

Please don't mention it.

No, Calculus, Cuthbert Calculus.

You see, here we are. One more floor . . .

It's in here . . .

Yes, that's a new device for putting bubbles in soda-water . . .

And that's a clothes-brushing machine.

Not a bad gadget, eh?

No, a clothes-brushing machine. It's one of my latest inventions.

RRRR ☆ OUCH

OW

OOH

The clothes are sucked into the middle of the machine, where they have a stiff brushing for half a minute. Then they come out, as good as new . . .

Billions of bilious blue blistering barnacles!!

Let me go! I'll tell him what I think of his practical joke!

You're going to buy me a new outfit, do you hear?

That? . . . Yes, it's for brushing clothes.

But this is even more ingenious. Because I have so little room and my bed gets in the way . . .

. . . I designed the wall-bed.

You Bashi-bazouk! Look what you've done now!

You bragging nitwit, you! Look!

How do I close it up again? There...

Between ourselves, I wouldn't have expected such childish pranks from them. They looked quite sensible...

And here's my apparatus for exploring the   sea-bed.

As you can see for yourselves, it's a kind of small submarine. It is powered by an electric motor, and has oxygen supplies for two hours' diving...

Now I'll show you how the apparatus works...

?   CRACK

I can't understand it!... It's sabotage! No sir, I said it's sabotage!... Someone has sabotaged my machine!

We are extremely sorry, Professor Calculus, extremely sorry, but your machine will not do.

For two? You'd like a two-seater?

No, Professor Calculus, I said your machine won't do for us!

Oh, good!

Well, gentlemen, that's agreed. I'll make another smaller one. It will be ready in eight days' time . . .

Some days later . . .

Well, we're all ready to start – at least, if we can find a diving-suit. I've spent three days hunting through marine stores, and I still haven't unearthed one.

I say, look there!

Great snakes! Let's go and see . . .

FOR SALE
Complete Diving Equipment, as new

We'd like to see the diving equipment, please.

The diving-suit? Please follow me.

There . . .

Beware, young fellow, beware! Money is the root of all evil!

?

Why . . . why do you say that?

Why? . . . Because I see that you intend to go treasure-hunting . . .

You see that? Where can you see it?

I read it I your face.

In my face? . . . But . . . but . . . what's unusual about my face? Tintin, can you see anything?

Well, I . . .

Blistering barnacles!

It's horrible! . . . What's happened to me? . . .

Nothing, Captain! It's just that you were looking in a concave mirror! And here's a convex one!

Thank goodness!

But here's another mirror . . . I'll just reassure myself!

Oh!

Seven years of bad luck!

And two pounds for the mirror!

You can take it from me: I'm telling you the truth: there's no such thing as buried treasure nowadays . . .

Never mind that. How much is the diving-suit?

Ten pounds.

All right. We'll have it collected this afternoon. Shall we go, Captain?

Remember what I said, my lad. You won't find any treasure!

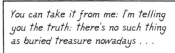

Next day . . .

SIRIUS

Good morning, Captain. All well?

No, bad!

Yes, bad. Very bad . . . I'm ill . . . 'Flu, I expect . . . And I've been thinking . . . I . . . well . . . briefly, to put it in a nut-shell, I'm not going!

!

You can't be serious!

Perfectly serious. I'm not superstitious, but to break a mirror on the eve of a voyage . . . No, definitely, I'm not going!

Hello!

Bad news, my friends. We've just heard that Max Bird has escaped!

What did I tell you? . . . A good start, isn't it? . . .

Yes, that troublesome antique dealer – he managed to give two policemen the slip when he was being taken for questioning.

That's bad . . .

There's a letter for you, Captain.

For me? . . . What's this about?

Billions of bilious blue blistering barnacles!

Is it bad news, Captain?

Read for yourself! It's ghastly!

DOCTOR A. LEECH

Dear Captain,
I have considered your case, and conclude that your illness is due to poor liver condition.
You must therefore undergo the following treatment:
DIET – STRICTLY FORBIDDEN:
All acoholic beverages (wine, beer, cider, spirits, cocktails,

Good-day, gentlemen! I hope I'm not intruding?

No? Well, I'm happy to tell you my machine is ready now.   When may I come aboard?

You can't come aboard! We aren't interested in your machine!

Tomorrow?

No not tomorrow! Never!

Today? . . . Good. I'll go and fetch it at once.

Blistering barnacles! You may be deaf, but you aren't blind, are you?

WE ARE <u>NOT</u> INTERESTED IN YOUR MACHINE!

That's that! Now he understands!

Let's hope so.

Captain, is what Tintin says really true? He's just told us you've decided not to go. It seems you broke a mirror and are afraid . . .

Afraid?

Me, afraid? . . . Afraid of what? . . . Afraid of whom? . . . Afraid of you, perhaps? Captain Haddock fears nothing! You understand? We weigh anchor at dawn tomorrow, no matter what anyone says! . . .

OUCH! . . .

At last we are on our way, Snowy.

Tintin!

A radio message . . .

"Port Commander to Captain SIRIUS. Reduce speed. Motor boat coming out to you." What can this mean?

Look! . . . There's a motor boat coming now.

I can't quite see the passenger; but it'd better not be Professor Calculus!

Thomson and Thompson! What are they coming aboard for?

Hello! We're coming with you!

Coming with us? . . .

Yes, we've had orders to protect you.

Protect us? Is someone threatening us? . . .

Yes, you are in danger. Max Bird, the antique dealer, was seen last night skulking near the SIRIUS. He may try to take his revenge.

Just let him try! He'll find out . . .

Maybe, maybe. But anyway, now we are aboard you will be able to feel that you are perfectly safe.

To be precise: perfectly safe.

We shall see . . . Meanwhile we must find you a berth. Let's see . . . We've a couple of spare bunks for'ard. Will that do?

Yes, thanks!

Captain! . . . Captain!

Captain, I can't stand it!

What?

This thieving Snowy - he's stolen a whole box of biscuits!

No? . . .

Snowy? . . .

Yes, Snowy! I saw him just now near the galley!

Snowy! . . . Where is the wretched animal?

Snowy? . . . SNOWY? . . .

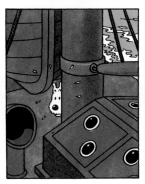

I can't see him, the scoundrel! But don't worry, I'll see that it doesn't happen again . . .

Good.

Er . . . our cabin is for'ard, isn't it?

Yes, for'ard.

We'll change at once, and mix discreetly with the ship's company . . .

Good idea!

We must behave like old sea-dogs . . .

For a start, we'd better learn to chew tobacco. All old sea-dogs chew a quid. Here, have one of these . . .

What do we do, Captain? We're bearing down on that fishing fleet . . .

Give a blast on the siren; that'll warn them.

TOOOOOT

Goodness! . . . My tobacco! . . .

Mine . . . mine too . . . I swallowed it! . . .

Next day . . .

This has got to stop! . . . Yes, it's got to stop!

Yes, Captain. Yesterday it was a box of biscuits! This morning a whole chicken has disappeared!

The wretched dog!

Snowy! . . . Snowy! . . . Where's he hiding? . . . Snowy!

Snowy! . . . Snowy! . . .

Snowy! . . . Snowy! . . . Where on earth can he be hiding? . . .

You really saw him make off with the chicken?

Well, I didn't exactly see him, but I supposed . . .

You supposed! . . . You supposed! . . . Don't you accuse anyone of anything unless you have proof! . . . Besides, how do we know you didn't eat the chicken yourself? . . .

That evening . . .

Good night. You might just keep an eye on Snowy.

Don't worry. I'll watch him! Good night Captain . . .

THIEF!

SAME TO YOU

Crumbs! That's the two detectives . . .

What's going on here? . . .

! !

It's him, Tintin! . . . He's stolen my pillow!

That's not true! It's him – he's taken one of my blankets!

Aren't you ashamed, at your age? Quarrelling over such trifles! Now, that's all over, isn't it?

Now let's go to bed!

Billions of blistering barnacles!

?

What's the matter, Captain?

The matter? Blistering barnacles, my bottle of whisky has vanished!

Vanished? Someone must be worried about your health and is keeping you to your diet . . .

You can laugh! . . . But if I catch the crook, he's in for a rough time!

We'll investigate it in the morning. Now let's go to bed. I'm dead tired. Good night!

You go to sleep if you like. I know what I'm going to do.

NO

NO ENTRY

OLD SCOTCH WHISKY

Thundering typhoons!

OLD SCOTCH WHISKY

NO ENTRY

THUMP THUMP THUMP

Tintin, Tintin, come quickly! . . . There's not a moment to lose!

We're going to blow up! . . . There's a bomb in the hold! . . .

I went down to the hold to open a case of whisky. And instead of whisky I found a bomb there! . . .

Here we are . . . Careful!

In here . . . Look . . .

NO ENTRY

Careful! . . . Don't go near it!

I must. We've got to get to the bottom of this . . .

Well? . . .

Steel plates!

Steel plates? . . .

NO ENTRY

You're right, by thunder! . . . Then it's not a bomb after all? . . .

Definitely not. Look, we'll open another case . . .

Blistering barnacles! More steel plates!

And in this one . . .

More steel plates!

Steaming blood! There's not a drop of whisky aboard! If I catch the monster who played this trick on us, he'll be in for a rough time! . . .

Come on, Captain. We'll try and solve this mystery in the morning . . .

Next day . . .

Anyway, we can't accuse Snowy any more. Some biscuits, even a chicken perhaps. But not a bottle of whisky!

OH!

Great snakes! ... He ... he ... why, he's drunk!

Snowy, what have you done? Pooh! Your breath smells of whisky!

Now come on! ... Show us where you found the whisky ...

All right ... You ... you want a d-d-d-drink too?

Look!

See, the bottle must have smashed up there. Let's investigate.

There!

Blistering barnacles! If I ever catch him!

Sh! ... Listen ...

ZZZ ... ZZZ ... ZZZ ...

Someone is asleep in this life-boat!

Impossible: the lashings are secure ... At least ...

Blistering barnacles! The lashings are free this side! There's someone in this life-boat!

Thundering typhoons!

ZZZ . . . ZZZ . . . ZZZ . . .

BISCUITS

Billions of bilious blue blistering barnacles! Get up, you! . . .

My whisky, you wretch! . . . What have you done with my whisky? Thundering typhoons, answer me! . . . Where's my whisky?

I must confess, I did sleep rather badly. But I hope you will give me a cabin . . .

A cabin! . . . I'll give you a cabin! . . . I'm going to stow you in the bottom of the hold for the rest of the voyage, on dry bread and water! . . . And my whisky? . . . Where's my whisky?

It's on board, of course!

It's on board! . . . Heaven be praised!

Naturally it is in separate pieces . . .

In separate pieces . . . My whisky is in separate pieces?

Of course, it is a little smaller than the first one, but nevertheless it was too big to pass unnoticed. So I had to dismantle it and pack all the parts in the cases . . .

But what about the whisky out of those cases! Tell me! Is it still ashore? . . .

Oh no!

No, no. It was night before you sailed. The cases were still on the quay, ready to be embarked. I took out all the bottles they contained, and put the pieces of my machine in their place . . .

Wretch! . . . Ignoramus! . . . Abominable Snowman! . . . I'll throw you overboard! Overboard, d'you hear? . . .

Thank you, Captain, thank you very much! It's just what I expected from you . . . Such a kind welcome! You'll see - you won't regret it.

Some days later . . .

SIRIUS

Look. We have reached the position indicated by the parchments. We should soon see the island off which the UNICORN sank . . .

Isn't the island marked on any charts?

No, but that sometimes happens with small, unimportant islands. Come on, we'll try to spot it . . .

I can't see anything yet . . . Can you? . . .

Nothing.

Can you see anything? . . .

Not yet. But there's a bottle of champagne for the first one to sight land!

Over there!

Where's the island? . . . I can't see anything . . .

It was, Captain. A shark, I know it was! I saw one, I really did!

Still no sign . . . It's very strange . . .

What's the name of the island?

How should I know? . . . It's not marked on any of the charts.

Oh? . . . But you are sure we're near it?

Positive! I plotted the position yesterday at noon.

Yes, I see. But . . . er . . . supposing you made a mistake in your calculations . . .

!?

Oh, so I made a mistake in my calculations, did I? . . . All right: they're on my table. Go and check them! . . . Yes, you! Now! Go on! Check them!

Tell me, Captain, was that a fish jumping out of the water just now?

No, it was a grand piano!

Ah, I didn't think it could have been a fish . . .

A few minutes later . . .

You must forgive me, Captain, but there really is a little mistake in your calculations. Look, this is where we are exactly . . .

You are right . . . I have made a mistake. Gentlemen, please take off your hats . . .

Why must we take off our hats, Captain? . . .

Sh! . . .

? ?

Now . . .

But Captain, tell us what you mean . . .

I mean, gentlemen, that according to your calculations we are now standing inside Westminster Abbey!

Thousands of thundering typhoons! Where's that miserable island got to?

I'm beginning to think Sir Francis Haddock was pulling our legs.

I'm beginning to think so too!

We'll soon see! It's almost noon. We'll take a sight. I'll go and fetch my sextant.

That's it . . . Let's go in, and I'll work it out . . .

The figures given in the parchments were latitude 20°37'42" North, longitude 70°52'15" West. Here's our position now; the same latitude, longitude 71°2'29" West.

So we've already passed the right point, and yet we saw nothing . . . I simply can't understand it!

Captain, I think I've got it!

!

What do you mean?

Well, the meridian from which you calculated the degrees of longitude was of course the Greenwich meridian . . .

You don't suppose I used one in Timbuctoo!

No, wait. Supposing Sir Francis Haddock used a French chart - he easily could have done. Then zero would be on the Paris meridian - and that lies more than two degrees east of Greenwich!

Blistering barnacles, that's an idea! You may be right! Perhaps we are too far to the west. We'll go back on our tracks . . .

Coxswain at the wheel! . . . Helm hard a-port! . . . Midships! . . . Steer due east.

?

Captain, what is happening? . . . We seem to be turning back.

Yes, Professor Calculus, we're turning back.

Oh, that's all right then . . . I was afraid we were turning back.

How easy it is to be mistaken. I'd have sworn we'd turned back.

That evening . . .

There it is at last! Our treasure island!

It's too late to go ashore tonight. We'll drop anchor, and tomorrow we'll explore the island . . .

Right! . . .

Next morning . . .

Haul the boat up the beach. I'm going to reconnoitre.

24

BANG

Crumbs! What's happened to him?

Captain, what was it? Are you hurt?

No. I stubbed my toe against that thing and fell over. That's how the gun went off . . .

OW! OW!

Keep calm! Keep calm!

YOW!

Here . . .

YEOW!

YOW!

YEOW!

Oh, leave them . . . Come and help me dig up this piece of wood. It intrigues me.

Hello, what have they found?

These are the remains of the jolly boat in which Sir Francis Haddock once came ashore on this island . . .

This certainly proves that we're nearing our goal. Red Rackham's treasure is out there at the bottom of the sea! . . . But now, shoes on, everyone, and let's carry on!

WOOAH!

That's Snowy! . . . He ran on ahead! . . .

? !

Where did you get that bone from Snowy? . . . Here, show us where you found it.

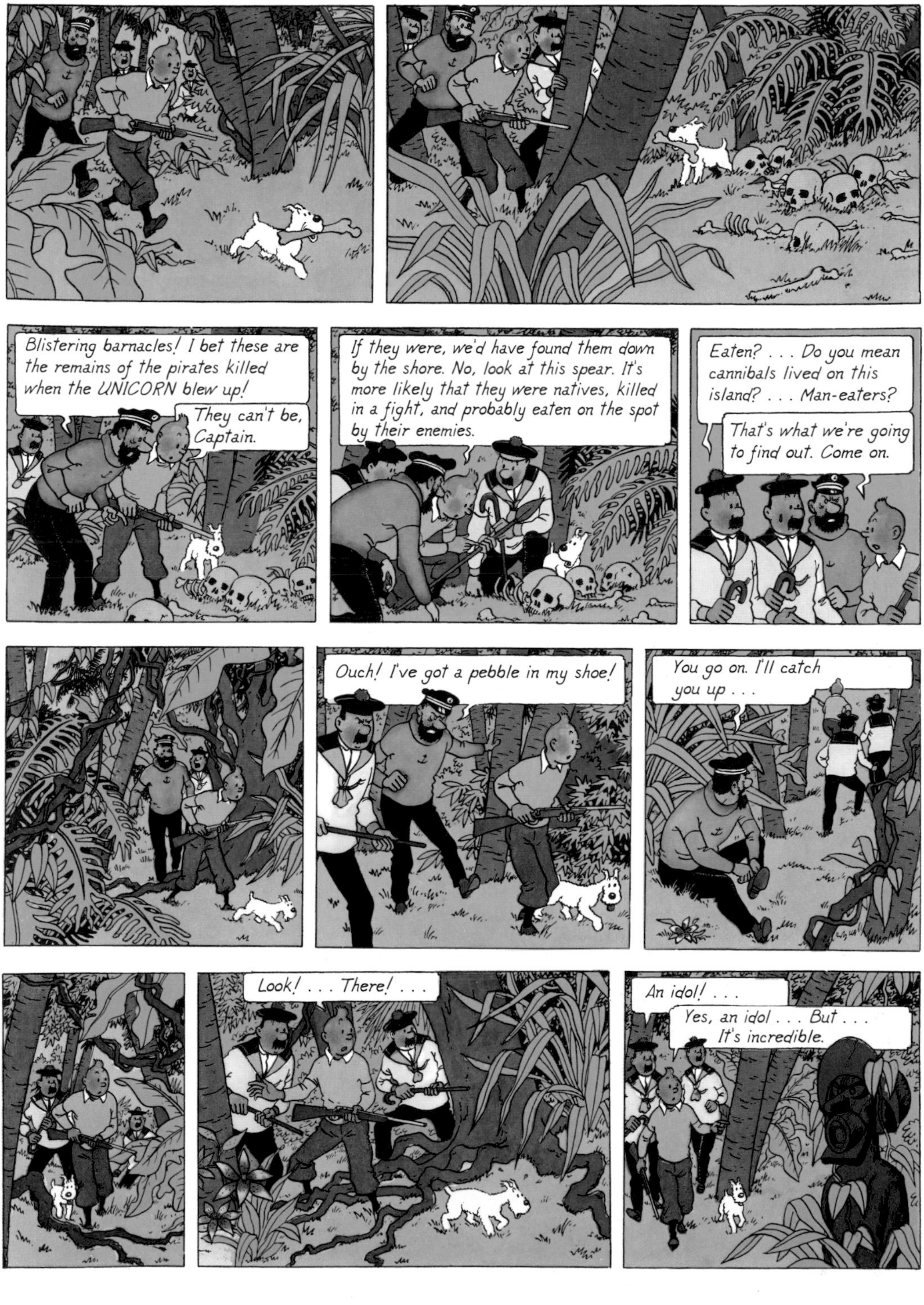
Blistering barnacles! I bet these are the remains of the pirates killed when the UNICORN blew up!
They can't be, Captain.
If they were, we'd have found them down by the shore. No, look at this spear. It's more likely that they were natives, killed in a fight, and probably eaten on the spot by their enemies.
Eaten? . . . Do you mean cannibals lived on this island? . . . Man-eaters?
That's what we're going to find out. Come on.
Ouch! I've got a pebble in my shoe!
You go on. I'll catch you up . . .
Look! . . . There! . . .
An idol! . . .
Yes, an idol . . . But . . . It's incredible.

My word! It's meant to be Sir Francis Haddock!

Look at that mouth! His voice must have made an enormous impression on the natives. I can just imagine their faces the first time they heard him shout: "Ration my rum!"

RRRATION MY RRRUM!

What's the matter, Captain?

Who shouted like that?

What? . . . Wasn't it you?

No, it wasn't me! Thundering typhoons!

Yes, it's Sir Francis Haddock.

RRRATION MY RRRUM!

It came from over there.

Not a soul!

This island is h-h-haunted, Captain. Let's hurry back t-t-to the sh-sh-ship.

To b-b-be precise: I-let's hurry back t-t-to the sh-sh-ship.

Pithecanthropus! . . . Pockmark! . . .

Pockmark yourself, you gibbering ghost!

Come out if you dare, Polynesian! . . . Cannibal! . . . Iconoclast! . . .

Nincompoop! . . . Ruffian! . . . Baboon!

Up there! . . .

Baboon!

Squawking popinjay!

Sea-gherkin!

Pickled herring!

Blistering barnacles! Parrots!!

Yes, parrots! From generation to generation your ancestor's vocabulary has been handed down!

Pockmark! . . . Freshwater swabs! . . . Bully! . . .

Me, a bully? You called me a bully did you? . . .

I'll show you what I'm made of!

Here's a coconut to cut your cackle, iconoclasts!

Ooh, my back!

Wait, I'll rub it for you.

Your gun! . . . Give me your gun! . . . I'm going to turn them into parrot soup.

Hey, Captain, calm yourself. After all, they're only parrots!

Bandits!

Forget about them, Captain. Let's go on.

You're right. Come on, let's go.

My gun! . . . Who has taken my gun? . . .

I only left it there for a moment . . .

Perhaps it fell into the bush?

Got it?

No . . . It's vanished completely!

Blue blistering . . .

Sh! . . . Listen!

What's that noise?

Crooee! . . . Crooee! . . . Crooee! . . .

Crooee! . . . Crooee! . . .

Blistering baboons! . . . Monkeys! . . . Gibbons! . . . Orang-outangs! . . . Give us back that gun, cercopithecuses!

That's no use, Captain. Leave it to me. I'll frighten them.

Hand's up! . . . Bang! . . . Bang! . . . Bang!

Hey, don't do that!

That's done it! . . . They've dropped the gun! . . . look, here it comes . . .

Very smart, weren't you, eh? . . . Look! . . . Another inch lower, and that would have been the end of Captain Haddock!

Anyway, all's well that ends well! . . . Shall we go back now, Captain? . . . We know the island is uninhabited.

Good idea. Let's go.

Thundering typhoons! I just remembered!

The idol! . . . Are we going to leave it here?

Ah! What pleasant visions
haunt me
As I gaze upon the sea!
All the old romantic legends,
All my dreams, come
back to me . . .

Look out! . . .
A shark! . . .

Thundering typhoons! . . . It almost
had my hand off!

Look there's another! . . . And
there . . . and there . . .

Quick, the gun! I'll tell
them a thing or two,
the brutes!

BING

You know, Captain, I'm beginning
to think Professor Calculus's
machine may come in very handy
for us . . .

Next day . . .

You've made up your mind?

Yes . . . Professor Calculus has explained exactly how his machine works. It'll be all right . . .

Stop! . . . Just a minute! . . .

I forgot to tell you. When you locate the wreck, press the little red button on the left of the instrument panel. That releases a small canister attached underneath the machine. It is full of a substance that gives off thick smoke when it comes into contact with water. That will show us where the wreck lies.

A little red button? . . . Right!

No, red! A little red button . . . You've got it? Good . . . Well, goodbye, and good luck!

There he goes: he's dived.

This is fun, eh Snowy?

Golly, what a lot of water!

Let's hope nothing goes wrong . . .

Gone long? Why, it's only ten minutes since he dived . . .

Hello, what's the matter? . . . The engine's stopped . . . We aren't moving any more!

?!

Thing's look bad, Snowy! Our propeller is entangled in the weeds!

We'll try and free ourselves by going into reverse . . .

It's no good! The propeller is completely jammed . . . and the engine has stalled!

Well, Snowy my boy, how do we get out of this?

There's only one thing to do: we'll release the smoke-canister. Then at least they'll know where we are . . . There, we press the little red button here . . .

That's it . . .

Look! . . . Look! . . . Smoke! . . . He's found the wreck of the UNICORN!

There, Professor Calculus! . . . Look! . . . Smoke! . . . He's found the wreck!

OH!

Captain, look there! . . . Look! . . . No, over there! Smoke! . . . He's found the wreck!

Patience, Snowy! . . . It won't be long before someone comes to rescue us.

Ahoy there! . . . Lower the dinghy! . . . We'll drop a buoy over the spot Tintin has marked.

There's the buoy . . .

. . . And there's the underwater viewing instrument.

It worries me a bit that Tintin hasn't come up again . . .

No, but I was a great sportsman in my youth . . .

. . . And that accounts for the athletic figure I still have . . .

Hm? . . .

To be quite honest, no . . . It was mostly walking . . .

Let's see . . .

Thundering typhoons! . . . It's not the wreck! . . . It's Tintin!

Wonderful! Quick, let me look . . .

Oh, Columbus! . . . The propeller has been fouled by weeds! . . . How can we save him?

x

35

Really, Captain! Your eyes have deceived you! It's not the wreck, it is Tintin. He can't resurface . . .

Your confounded contraption! I should never have let him go down!

May drown? Well, he had enough oxygen for two hours. He's got . . . Let's see . . . yes, he has just enough for another ten minutes!

I hope they hurry! It's getting more and more difficult to breathe . . .

What can we do? How can we save him?

Lower a diver? . . . No, by the time we'd got one equipped and ready, Tintin would be dead . . .

No, I've go an idea. Take the anchor! . . . The anchor used for mooring the buoy!

The anchor? What for? . . .

Of course! . . . We'll try and hook it on to the submarine. Then we'll pull on the rope until the weeds break . . .

That's it! Let it down . . . Lower . . . lower . . . lower . . . gently . . .

An anchor! . . . They're going to try to hook me. Quick, empty the ballast tanks, that'll help them . . .

He's understood. He's emptied the ballast tanks to lighten the submarine . . . A bit to the left, Captain . . . Good . . . Now, pull!

Ah, they've got it! . . . I'm saved! . . . Just in time! I'm suffocating.

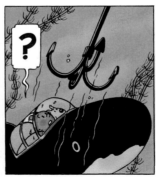

?

Missed! . . . The anchor hadn't caught properly. Lower it again . . . down . . . stop! A bit to the right . . . now to the left . . . Pull it up gently . . .

Pull! . . . Pull! . . . For goodness' sake pull!

Pull! . . . Go on, pull!

Thundering typhoons, I'm trying to! What do you think I'm doing? Playing the cornet?

Billions of blue blistering barnacles! I hope there aren't any sharks about.

Fresh air! . . . Fresh air at last! . . .

Hooray! . . . He's safe! . . . Hip-hip-hooray!

All's well! . . . The Captain has climbed back into the boat . . . He's salvaged the buoy . . . hauled the anchor inboard . . . thrown a lifeline to Tintin . . . Ah, here they come . . .

Well, our friend Tintin had a narrow escape!

You are wrong, I assure you. Weeds jammed the propeller. You'll see when we're back on board.

You see? . . . It's just as I said. Weeds . . .

Really? I thought they were weeds . . .

Weeds or no weeds, I don't set foot in that thing again! . . .

Fine. Get it ready. Snowy and I are setting out again immediately!

Let's hope he doesn't run into any more trouble this time . . .

What shall I do? Tell him . . . or not?

I've made up my mind . . .

I . . . Captain . . . I've bad news for you.

Bad news for me?

No, bad news for you, very bad news . . . I'm afraid the UNICORN is not here . . . Look . . .

What's that gadget, eh?

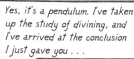

Yes, it's a pendulum. I've taken up the study of divining, and I've arrived at the conclusion I just gave you . . .

All from that whatsit?

Yes, much further west . . . You'll see. My pendulum will begin swinging from east to west . . . Look, it's started . . .

You see? . . . It's swinging westwards. The UNICORN will be found in that direction.

Look there, Captain! Smoke!

And look, there's the submarine surfacing! . . . This time we've got it! . . . He's found the wreck!

Have you found it?

Westwards . . . It's still westwards.

Yes. I've found the UNICORN! . . . You can prepare the diving equipment!

You're sure you'll be all right? . . .

Certain! I'll do everything exactly as you told me . . .

Good! Now, don't forget . . . If you want to come up, jerk the line twice . . . In an emergency, give a series of quick jerks.

Right!

Come on, pump hard!

We are!

?

Wooah! Wooah!

Wooah! Wooah!

That's it, he's touched bottom . . .

So this is the UNICORN!

Crumbs! What's happening? The air supply has stopped! ...

Thundering typhoons! What are you two doing there, instead of pumping?

Us? We're resting . . . it's tiring work, you know.

You infernal impersonations of abominable snowmen! Pump for your lives! . . . Faster!

Whew! . . . That's better! . . . Now the air's coming again. That gave me quite a fright . . .

Excuse me, Captain, but I don't understand . . . Since the UNICORN is not here, why has Tintin gone down?

He's picking daisies down below!

?

Having a row? I don't see a boat?

Two jerks on the line! He wants to come up! I'm sure he must have found something!

Heave-ho! . . . Heave-ho!

Here he is.

What has he got?

A gold cross, encrusted with precious stones! . . . and a cutlass! . . . I say, this cross is superb!

We've made a good start, eh?

Now why did he tell me that Tintin had gone for a row?

Yes, it's a good start. But this is nothing to what else we shall find. You'll see. I'm going down myself, this time.

By the way . . . er . . . any sign of sharks?

No, none at all.

Here's your helmet.

Good.

Ow! . . . OOH! . . . OW!

Whatever's the matter?

Blistering barnacles! My beard!

!

There, now your beard is inside.

Good. You can close my helmet now. Keep an eye on that pumping.

Aha! Now to find the treasure! . . .

A few minutes later . . .

A series of jerks! . . . The danger signal! . . .

Hurry! Hurry! Pull him up! . . . Something frightful must have happened!

Let's hope that it's not a shark . . .

At last!

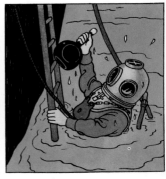

A bottle? What can that mean? . . .

A bottle of rum, my friends! . . . Jamaica rum, and it's more than two hundred and fifty years old! . . . Just you taste it!

GLUG GLUG GLUG

GLUG GLUG

Mm! . . . It's wonderful! . . . It's absolutely w-w-wonderful! Y-y-you taste it! . . . Yes, yes, that's f-f-for you! . . . I'm g-g-going st-st-st-straight back to g-get a-a-another f-for m-myself . . .

That beats everything! He's gone in without his helmet!

Billions of bilious blue blistering barnacles! Those two jelly-fishes forgot to pump again! . . .

Sea-gherkins! . . . Freshwater swabs! . . . Ectoplasms! . . . Bashi-bazouks! . . .

But . . . but it wasn't us, you . . .

Silence! You were told to pump, then pump, by thunder!

It's no use drying yourself, Captain. You must empty your suit first . . . Take it off now.

Take it off? . . . Never! . . . Never! . . .

I'll rest a minute and go down again . . .

You see? . . . I told you so! . . . Your suit is full of water . . . We'll have to empty it.

There! Now you can go down again, if you still want to. But don't forget your helmet this time!

Off we go! . . . As for you, my hearties, just you keep on pumping until you're ordered to stop! . . . You understand? . . .

Yes, yes, we're pumping . . .

There he goes now . . .

The same evening . . .

A good day's work! . . . First that cross, and then . . . more important, all this rum! . . . Fine stuff eh?

Yes, but I'd sooner have found the treasure.

Oh, we'll find that tomorrow, won't we Professor Calculus? . . .

Perhaps, but I'm inclined to think it is rum.

CHEEEP! CHEEEP CHEEEP

Ssh!

It sounds like a bird . . .

CHEEEP

I'd say it was the squeak of a badly greased wheel . . .

Let's see. I want to set my mind at rest.

There, Captain. It's the pump making that noise.

CHEEEP
CHEEEP

What d'you think you're doing at this hour?

You never ordered us to stop pumping, Captain. So here we are, pumping.

To be precise: we're pumping.

Off to bed, nitwits! You'll have plenty more pumping, believe me!

The next morning . . .

Something tells me Tintin is going to find the treasure this morning.

Another bottle of rum! . . . I'll leave it there for the Captain.

Hello, I wonder what we've got here?

A casket! Great snakes! Can it be Red Rackham's treasure?

I'll go straight up, and see what's inside this casket!

Goodness, he's swallowed it! And he's coming back for me!

He's grabbed the casket!

He's coming again. What can I do? If only I had a weapon.

Perhaps this bottle will help . . .

Quick, back against this old rib. Then he won't sever my air-pipe . . .

Good heavens, what a blow!

Thank goodness my suit isn't damaged.

?

My stars! He's drunk!

Now he's sleeping it off, I suppose. Here's my chance to try and recover the casket.

Two jerks on the line! He wants us to pull him up.

Heave-ho! Heave-ho! . . . You wait! He'll be bringing us the treasure.

Thundering typhoons! Why does he have to struggle so?

?

Blistering barnacles, a shark! What a fellow; he's caught a shark! . . . But what does he want us to do with it?

The best thing is to ask him.

Of course! . . . Lower another line to him, and pull him up.

Now, up I go. I wonder what the Captain will say!

Well, what's the meaning of this little joke?

Little joke? . . . Just cut open that shark, Captain, and you'll see.

In any case, I believe the fins are particularly tasty . . .

A few minutes later . . .

Captain! . . . Captain! . . . Look what we found in the shark's stomach!

A casket! . . . A casket! . . . Red Rackham's treasure! Red Rackham's treasure!! . . . Here it is at last!

Quick, into my cabin!

Hm! . . . Not so easy! It's all rusted up.

It's no good, you'll snap the blade. Better try this case opener.

Good idea. Hold it tight, you two.

Go on! Go on: don't worry, we're holding it . . .

Got it! . . .

CRACK

Billions of bilious blue blistering barnacles in a thundering typhoon! . . . It's not the treasure!

These are old documents, half eaten away by damp!

Documents? Fine! And what am I supposed to do with documents?

Come now, Captain, don't lose heart! . . . We'll continue our search.

What's the use?

That's it! . . . I've got it!

These are old documents! . . . Definitely! . . . Old documents!

That chap will drive me crazy!

And you there? Thundering typhoons, what are you doing?

Me? . . . You can see - I'm helping my colleague to go down . . . Oh, don't worry. I've watched carefully how you do it . . .

What about the pump? The pump works by itself, I suppose?

I'll work the pump, nincompoop! . . . Then at least I'll know he's safe.

Thundering typhoons! What's that over there, on the deck?

The weighted boots! . . . He's forgotten the weighted boots!

A fortnight later . . .

Here we are, pumping as usual . . .

As usual . . .

Blistering barnacles! You can stop pumping! Can't you see that Tintin's come up?

Well?

Nothing . . . Nothing at all! I've been carefully through all that's left of the poop . . .

It's just as I said: we aren't going to find it.

Come on, Captain, you . . .

Tell me, what is that cross over there?

A cross? Where can you see a cross?

No, a cross . . . that cross over there on the island.

It certainly is a cross, isn't it? . . .

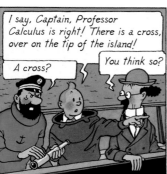

I say, Captain, Professor Calculus is right! There is a cross, over on the tip of the island!

A cross?

You think so?

Thundering typhoons! It is indeed a cross!

Really? I'd have sworn it was a cross!

Hooray! . . . Hip-hip-hip-hoo-ray! . . . I've got it!

?

Professor Calculus, Professor Calculus, you've saved us!

Let me waltz ♩♩ with you ♫, The whole ♩♩ night through ♫

Quickly, Captain! . . . Picks! . . . Shovels! . . . We're going back to the island.

Yes, Captain, the treasure lies there! You remember the words in Sir Francis Haddock's message: "then shines forth the Eagle's cross". There it is: the Eagle's cross!

Thundering typhoons! You're right!

Hooray! Thomson! . . . Thompson! . . . Fetch the picks and shovels! Hurry up! . . . Into the dinghy!

Well, Professor Calculus, we can never thank you enough!

It is rather rough . . .

No, I said it is thanks to you that we are going to find the treasure.

Oh . . . Well, I'm sure it's a cross!

Of course, of course it is a cross . . .

No? . . . D'you think so?

Baboon! Freshwater swab!

Hello, my old friend!

Hooray! Here it is!

Gentlemen, this is it, the Eagle's cross!

Well, what did I tell you? Is it or is it not a cross?

Why, what's the meaning of all these notches?

A calendar! When your ancestor was marooned – like Robinson Crusoe, he counted the days until he was rescued. Look: there's a small notch for weekdays, and a large one for Sundays . . .

To work, to work! I'll give a bottle of rum to whoever finds the treasure!

Are you . . . er . . . looking for something? . . .

!

Blistering barnacles, put away your pendulum; come and give us a hand instead!

Towards the west; yes, it does . . .

What can they be searching for like that?

But . . . no, it's impossible!

What? . . . What is so impossible?

That the treasure can be here!

W-w-what? . . . Why? . . .

Just think . . . Supposing Sir Francis Haddock left the UNICORN, carrying the treasure; why would he have buried it here, at the foot of this cross? . . . What would you have done in his place? On the day you left this island you'd have taken the treasure with you, wouldn't you?

But then . . .

Then? . . . Probably the treasure is still out there, under the sea! . . . And we've followed a false trail!

All because of that creature Calculus, blistering barnacles!

Yes, it's all your fault, you certified ignoramus!

Yes; I'm tired of telling you: it's further westwards!

Westwards! . . . Westwards! . . . I'll give you westwards!

OH!

Now your infernal pendulum's gone west, you Olympic athlete, you!

Wooah! Wooah!

Take that! . . . And that! . . . Now it's buried, pestilential pendulum!

There! . . . And don't mention it again! Come on now, we're going back!

He's furious!

What a good little doggie you are! . . .

Down, Snowy! ...No more games, now!

Is something bothering the Captain?. . . He seems to be rather worried!

Where have the Siamese twins got to?

Why, I thought they were behind us.

AHOY! THOMSON! THOMPSON!

No, no, please don't worry. The little dog brought it back for me.

Billions of blue blistering barnacles! This time I've had enough!

Captain! Captain!

Leave me alone! I've got to let fly at something!

Thousands of thundering typhoons! That's the lot, eh?

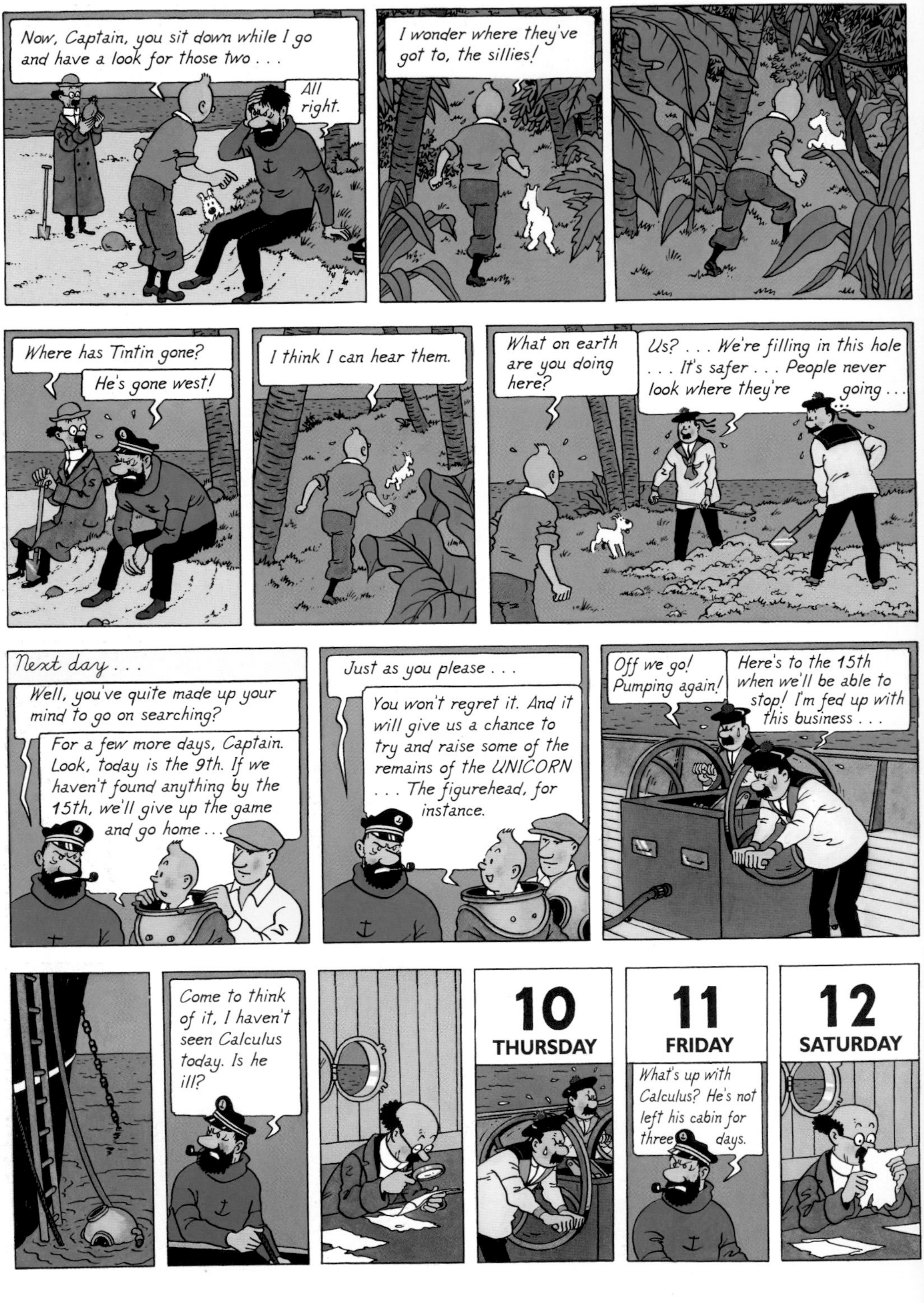

Now, Captain, you sit down while I go and have a look for those two . . .
All right.
I wonder where they've got to, the sillies!
Where has Tintin gone?
He's gone west!
I think I can hear them.
What on earth are you doing here?
Us? . . . We're filling in this hole . . . It's safer . . . People never look where they're going . . .
Next day . . .
Well, you've quite made up your mind to go on searching?
For a few more days, Captain. Look, today is the 9th. If we haven't found anything by the 15th, we'll give up the game and go home . . .
Just as you please . . .
You won't regret it. And it will give us a chance to try and raise some of the remains of the UNICORN . . . The figurehead, for instance.
Off we go! Pumping again!
Here's to the 15th when we'll be able to stop! I'm fed up with this business . . .
Come to think of it, I haven't seen Calculus today. Is he ill?
10 THURSDAY
11 FRIDAY
What's up with Calculus? He's not left his cabin for three days.
12 SATURDAY

13 SUNDAY

Still no luck, Captain...

14 MONDAY

15 TUESDAY

?

What... What's happening?... It looks as if...

Oh dear, I'm right!... I must warn the Captain!

Come on, Captain, don't let this upset you. It's bad luck, I know, but you must make the best of it...

Captain!... Captain!... The ship is sailing!

Well, what would you like it to do? Dance a jig?

Ah, I see now. At last you have realised that the UNICORN is not where you were looking; you are steering westwards. I understand...

I've had enough! Come with me!

You see that, eh? I suppose it's the figure-head of the TITANIC!

My word, it's a unicorn! But what about my pendulum, which swung to the west?... How extraordinary...

16 WEDNESDAY **17 THURSDAY** **18 FRIDAY** **19 SATURDAY** **20 SUNDAY** **21 MONDAY** **22 TUESDAY**

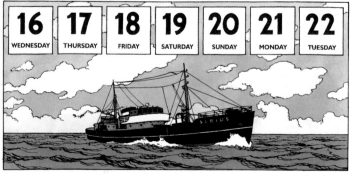

 RRRING RRRING

JULY 23 WEDNESDAY

Hello. Yes . . . "Daily Reporter" . . . Yes . . . What? The SIRIUS has docked? . . . Are you sure? . . . Good . . . Thanks!

Hello, is that you Rogers? . . . Go to the docks at once. The SIRIUS has just come in . . . I want a good story about her!

 Well, Captain, I'll say goodbye to you now. I'll have my submarine collected tomorrow morning.

All right. Good.

Now, please let me thank you, Captain. You have been so very kind.

Oh, it was nothing.

Yes, yes, Captain. Thanks to you. I shall always have unforgettable memories of my stay on board . . .

So shall I!

THUD

Er . . . excuse me . . . I missed a step!

Allow me to introduce myself: Ken Rogers of the "Daily Reporter".

"Daily Reporter"? Wasn't yours the paper that gave the news of our departure?

It was! . . . And we would like to publish a sensational article about your trip. May I ask you a few questions?

Of course . . .

I'm rather busy myself. This is my secretary, Mr Calculus; he will be happy to answer all your inquiries.

Delighted . . .

Now Mr Calculus, about the treasure . . . Oh . . . yes.

I'm sure you have it there, in the suitcase . . .

Thank you, I'll carry it myself.

I can understand that! . . . Now tell me, what does the treasure consist of?

No? . . . Not really? . . .

No, I asked you what was in the treasure you found. Was it gold? . . . Pearls? . . . Diamonds?

Incredible! I don't believe a word of it!

(56)

Look, Mr Calculus. I don't quite follow . . .

Of course! But let me give you a little advice: don't tell anyone!

And you may rely on me – I will keep this strictly between ourselves!

Well, Captain, our mission is completed. Because he knew we were aboard, Max Bird didn't dare interfere with your activities.

No doubt . . . You're going home now?

No, we're a bit tired . . . The journey, you know . . . and the pumping . . . We're going to spend a few days in the country with a farmer friend of ours.

Have a good holiday!

Now for the simple, healthy tasks of the countryside! No more pumping!

To be precise: no more pump-   ing!

. . . and when you've finished crushing the oats, you can have a turn at the chaff-cutter.

Some days later . . .

Good morning, Tintin.

Hello, Professor Calculus. What brings you here?

Very well, thank you. And you? . . . I've come to bring you the documents . . .

The documents? . . . What documents? . . .

No, the documents we found in the casket . . . Don't you remember? . . . I've tried to piece them together, sticking the fragments on sheets of paper. Some are illegible. Others, like that one, are comparatively easy   to decipher.

I believe that one will interest the Captain particularly.

Great snakes! I think so too!

Come on! We must see the Captain!

Charles the Second, by ye Grace of God King of England, desiring to reward Our trusty and beloved Knight Francis Haddock . . . Blistering barnacles!

The rest! Read the rest!

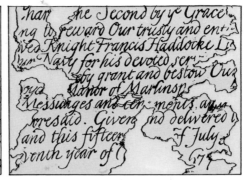

Thundering typhoons! Am I dreaming! It's Marlinspike Hall! . . . Marlinspike, my family estate! It's fantastic!

But you don't know the latest! Wait, you'll see . . .

Here . . . read this!

Well, what about that?

PROPER

JAMES BIDDUP & CO.

For Sale by Auction

ON SATURDAY,
9TH AUGUST

MARLINSPIKE HALL

This magnificent, beautifully appointed, and historic residence
...ensive parkland and

What about it? . . . Well, Captain, it's quite simple. Your family estate is for sale! . . . You must buy it back!

Buy it back? With what?

That's true . . . We need some money.

Heigh-ho! . . . If only we'd found that wretched treasure, there'd be no question.

May I please have a look too?

Of course.

!

Captain, Marlinspike Hall is for sale! . . . Look! We must buy it back!

Oh, yes?

Buy it back? . . . That's easy, eh? . . . What about the money? I suppose you've got the money, eh?

Oh, yes, money! That doesn't matter! . . .

That's all right! I have some money.

You? . . . You've got money? . . . That's nice for you! . . . Personally, I haven't any!

Quite! The government have paid me a large sum for the patent on my submarine. Thanks to you I was able to try it out. Now it's my turn to help you . . . Come along, we're going to buy your mansion.

HOUSE
FOR
SALE

HOUSE
is not
FOR
SALE

All's well that ends well! . . . You haven't found the treasure, but you have got back your family estate.

It is magnificent!

Wait, you haven't seen anything yet.

This is the room where I telephoned you.

Splendid!

SSH!

No . . . Nothing . . . I thought I heard footsteps . . .

Oh?

Well, it's a wonderful house! . . . My ancestor had good taste, didn't he? . . . Now what about those famous cellars you talked of? Where are they?

Come with me . . . I'll take you there.

Look! Here we are!

Thundering typhoons!

What a lot of junk! . . . All this junk!

Oh yes, the Bird brothers used this as a storeroom.

Look, that's St. John the Evangelist. We must be in an old chapel . . .

What do you think of it?

Incre— dible!

Sh! . . . This time I'm sure I heard a noise!

It's gone . . . The footsteps have stopped . . . It's queer. I wonder . . .

What?

Why, whatever's the matter? What is it?

Hooray!

The Eagle's cross! . . . "And then shines forth the Eagle's cross"! There it is . . . the Eagle's cross . . .

The Eagle's cross? . . . I can see a cross, but where is the Eagle?

There, in front of you!

Yes there, look! . . . St. John the Evangelist — who is always depicted with an eagle . . . And he's called the Eagle of Patmos — after the island where he wrote his Revelation . . . He's the Eagle! . . .

There's a globe!

And an eagle! . . . You're right! . . .

There, just on the spot given in the old parchment, is the island we went to! . . . Great snakes! The island's moving!

?

!?   !?

The treasure! . . . The treasure!! . . . Blistering treasures! It's Red Rackham's barnacles!

We've found it! . . . We've found it at last: Red Rackham's treasure! . . . Look! . . . Look!

It's stupendous! . . . Stupendous! . . . So Sir Francis Haddock did take the treasure with him when he left the UNICORN . . . And to think we were looking for it half across the world, when all the time it was lying here, right under our very noses . . .

Thundering typhoons, look at this! . . . Diamonds! . . . Pearls! . . . Emeralds! . . . Rubies! . . . Er . . . all sorts! . . . They're magnificent!

Sh! . . . Did you hear that?

Yes . . .

Listen . . . Footsteps! . . . Someone's coming towards the cellars . . .

Quick! Get hold of a weapon! We'll each hide behind a pillar . . .

Right! Come on!

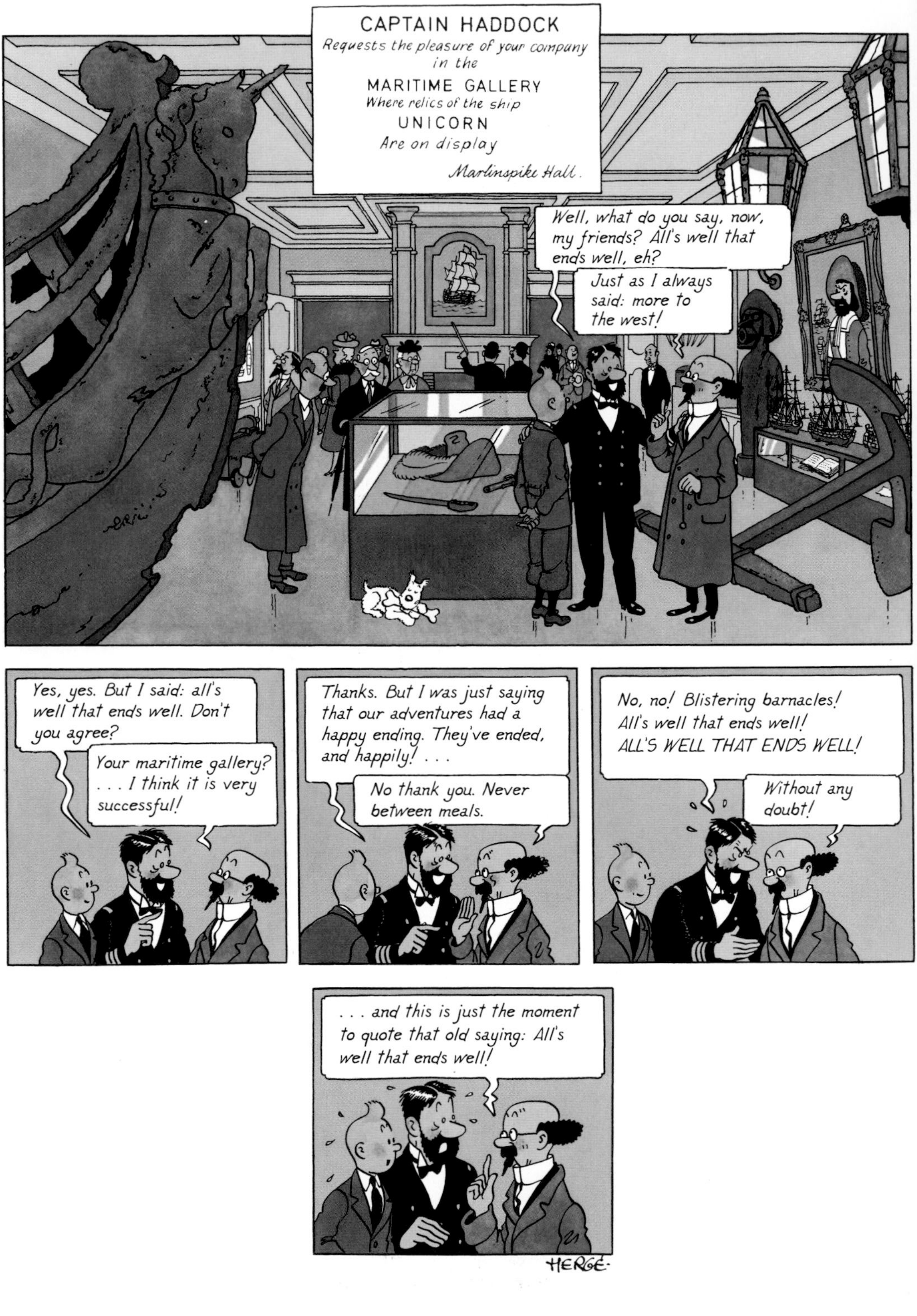
CAPTAIN HADDOCK
Requests the pleasure of your company
in the
MARITIME GALLERY
Where relics of the ship
UNICORN
Are on display
Marlinspike Hall.
Well, what do you say, now, my friends? All's well that ends well, eh?
Just as I always said: more to the west!
Yes, yes. But I said: all's well that ends well. Don't you agree?
Your maritime gallery? . . . I think it is very successful!
Thanks. But I was just saying that our adventures had a happy ending. They've ended, and happily! . . .
No thank you. Never between meals.
No, no! Blistering barnacles! All's well that ends well! ALL'S WELL THAT ENDS WELL!
Without any doubt!
. . . and this is just the moment to quote that old saying: All's well that ends well!
HERGÉ

THE REAL-LIFE INSPIRATION
BEHIND
TINTIN'S ADVENTURES

Written by Stuart Tett
with the collaboration of Studio Moulinsart.

Discover something new and exciting

HERGÉ

The archives

To write and draw stories with real clothes, buildings, cars and all kinds of other scenery in them, Hergé collected pictures and articles from newspapers and magazines.

As his collection grew, Hergé began using folders to classify the text and images by subject. In the end, his archives contained about 20,000 documents.

about Tintin and his creator Hergé!

TINTIN

At sea

Tintin loves traveling by boat, but the little reporter took to the water long before *Red Rackham's Treasure*. Hergé drew Tintin escaping from villains in a speedboat in his first adventure, *Tintin in the Land of the Soviets*.

THE TRUE STORY
...behind *Red Rackham's Treasure*

At the beginning of the story, Captain Haddock walks straight into a Morris column—a cylindrical advertising billboard—and bangs his head on a poster for the *Daily Reporter*. As if the captain wasn't angry enough with the newspaper already!

© Getty Images

A journalist for the *Daily Reporter* has written a story about the treasure hunt that Captain Haddock is about to go on with his friend Tintin. They could have done without all the attention!

The nosy journalist responsible can be seen on page 1. Bill—the cook on board the *Sirius*—realizes that someone is listening to their conversation and warns his friend that "These walls have ears."

Once upon a time…

At the time that Hergé wrote this story, Europe was at war and Belgium was occupied by enemy troops. The old proverb "the walls have ears" was very apt for a time when you had to be careful what you said, just in case the enemy's secret police were listening!

A determined visitor

Captain Haddock manages to scare off most of the visitors, but one of them—Professor Calculus—proves to be very stubborn!

There are two reasons for this:

1. The professor is extremely deaf, and cannot understand the repeated attempts made by Captain Haddock and Tintin to send him packing.
2. Professor Calculus has an exciting submarine that he is desperate to try out in the hunt for Red Rackham's treasure!

Once upon a time…

Professor Calculus shows Tintin and his friends around his laboratory. At the moment in March 1943 when Hergé was drawing the professor's submarine collapsing, the sale of Tintin books was also about to be sabotaged. Due to severe paper shortages in occupied Belgium, on March 31 there were no more Tintin books in stock!

Despite various difficulties, Captain Haddock and Tintin manage to find all the equipment they need. Thomson and Thompson come to visit them on the *Sirius*, the day before they are due to set sail. The ship is docked at a port and although it doesn't say so in the story, Hergé would certainly have had the port of Antwerp in mind. Antwerp is the main port in Belgium.

Once upon a time...

During World War II, Antwerp was under German control. Being a port, it was strategically important and on September 4, 1944, Allied forces captured Antwerp. The Allies were helped by the Belgian Resistance, who bravely and heroically sabotaged the retreating army's plans to destroy the port. When the Allies arrived, the port and facilities were intact!

© Musée royal de l'Armée, Bruxelles

Off we go!

Tintin and Captain Haddock set sail and begin their exciting treasure hunt. Now we are going to **Explore and Discover!**

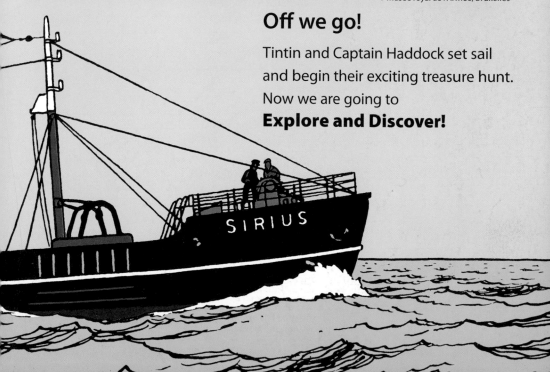

EXPLORE AND DISCOVER

Before they set off on their adventure, Tintin and Captain Haddock visit a basement shop with a diving suit for sale. Compare the picture below of the basement with a clipping from a German newspaper contained in Hergé's archives. The creator of Tintin was inspired by the cartoonist!

Berliner Illustrirte Zeitung   1939

... schüchtern und erwartungsvoll stieg ich in das Lokal hinunter. Eine richtige Seemannskneipe, ahoi!! Wrackstücke, Rettungsringe, Taucherhelme überall, und von der Decke her glotzten Haifische, die fürchterlichen Hyänen der Meere. Ich bat um ein Glas Bier. Es kam nicht. Etwas lauter bat ich noch einmal um ein Glas Bier, da ...

THE *SIRIUS*

For the maritime treasure hunt Captain Haddock borrows a ship called the *Sirius* from his friend Captain Chester (see *The Shooting Star*). Hergé based the *Sirius* on a real ship, a fishing trawler named the *John 0.88*. Hergé even commissioned a model of the ship!

THE *JOHN 0.88*

★ The *John 0.88* was built by Boël shipbuilders in Tamise, Belgium. The ship was launched in 1936.

★ At the outset of World War II the British Navy requisitioned the *John 0.88*. It continued to provide fish for the population of Great Britain.

★ In June 1941, the *John 0.88* was attacked by German fighter planes. Unfortunately, although the captain fired back with his machine gun, the ship was riddled with bullets and soon sank.

THE LOST ISLAND

Captain Haddock has double-checked his calculations, but where is the island? Tintin has the answer! Sir Francis Haddock must have used the Paris Meridian to pinpoint the island's location, but Captain Haddock is navigating by the Greenwich Meridan. They are too far west!

MERIDIANS

★ Each meridian, or line of longitude, is an imaginary line from the North Pole to the South Pole.

★ Together with lines of latitude, running around the Earth parallel to the Equator, meridians are used to pinpoint locations on the Earth's surface.

★ There are 360 degrees of meridians spanning the globe; the Prime Meridian starts at 0 degrees.

★ In 1884, at a conference in the USA, the Greenwich Meridian was chosen as the Prime Meridian, over the Paris Meridian!

That's it . . . Let's go in, and I'll work it out . . .

SQUAWK TALK!

The island is haunted by the ghost of Sir Francis Haddock! Or is it? Parrots have been passing down Sir Francis Haddock's colorful language from generation to generation. Now that they've met Captain Haddock, they might learn a bit more bad language!

Not only did he impress the parrots, but Captain Haddock's ancestor also appears to have impressed the natives on the island. They even made a statue of him! A Bamileke carving from Cameroon inspired Hergé as he created the statue of Sir Francis Haddock.

Private collection: Count Bauduin de Grunne, Wezembeek-Oppem

13

As he put more and more effort into making his stories realistic, the author of Tintin commissioned model makers and sculptors to create models of vehicles and objects that appeared in his comic strips. You have already seen the model of the *Sirius*, now check out the photo of Hergé below, in his office in Brussels!

© SOFAM/Robert Kayaert 1960

THE SHARK SUBMARINE

Tintin tries out Professor Calculus's shark submarine. Hergé was inspired by a picture of an experimental shark-shaped submarine, which he saw in a newspaper. Look at this photo from his archives. ▶

Weeds or no weeds, I don't set foot in that thing again! . . .

SNOWY'S LAST WORDS

This frame from page 38 shows the last time in this adventure that Snowy speaks! After doing a lot of talking in the first ten Tintin stories, from now on Tintin's faithful dog chats less and barks more, making way for Tintin's talkative friend Captain Haddock.

THE *UNICORN*

Tintin puts on a diving suit and leaves his friends behind on the decks of the *Sirius*. He has discovered the *Unicorn*!

Hergé's archives contain a breathtaking picture of divers exploring the shipwreck of the *Vasa*, which you can see on the opposite page.

THE *VASA*

★ The *Vasa* was a Swedish warship built between 1626 and 1628.

★ At the time it was built, the *Vasa* had the most powerful broadside in the world: it could fire 589 lbs of cannon balls from one side at once.

★ The *Vasa* was built top-heavy; in 1628 the ship sank to the bottom of the Baltic Sea, on its maiden voyage.

★ Thanks to the low salinity of the water in this area, the ship remained largely intact until it was salvaged in 1961.

STAFF ARTIST, Robert W. Nicholson
© NATIONAL GEOGRAPHIC SOCIETY

PROFESSOR CALCULUS

In *Red Rackham's Treasure*, Hergé intro-
duces a character who will become close
friends with Tintin and Captain Haddock
for the rest of the adventures: Professor
Calculus.

Professor Calculus is an eccentric scientist and inventor. He is hard of hearing, which leads to many funny misunderstandings.

The professor also claims to have been a sportsman
in his youth, which Captain Haddock refers to when
he impatiently calls Calculus an "Olympic athlete"!

Although he is a very capable scientist and engi-
neer, Professor Calculus also practices the unproven
method of divining, using a pendulum that succeeds
mainly in infuriating Captain Haddock.

Nevertheless, at the end of the adventure, we discover that there is an ele-
ment of truth to the professor's use of the pendulum when the treasure is
finally found in the west!

MODEL SCIENTIST

Hergé's model for Professor Calculus was a Swiss scientist named Auguste Piccard, who was a professor of physics at the University of Brussels from 1922 to 1954.

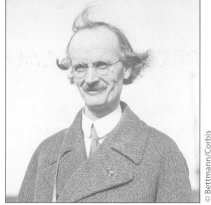

© Bettmann/Corbis

The *Trieste* bathyscaphe

AUGUSTE PICCARD

★ Professor Auguste Piccard was born in 1884 and died in 1962. He had a twin brother who was also a renowned scientist.

★ In 1931, Auguste Piccard took off in a balloon of his own design and traveled 10 miles up into the atmosphere, higher than anyone else had reached before.

★ Professor Piccard's son, Jacques Piccard, holds the record for the deepest dive in the ocean made by a human being. He made the descent in the *Trieste* bathyscaphe, which was also designed by his father!

Professor Calculus shares many character traits with the Swiss scientist, and even wears the same style of clothing as Piccard liked to wear. The main difference between the men is in size: Professor Calculus is much shorter. As Hergé himself said: "I made Calculus a mini-Piccard, otherwise I would have had to make the comic strip frames bigger!"

MARLINSPIKE HALL

Despite their best efforts, the team on board the *Sirius* does not manage to find Red Rackham's treasure. But they do find plenty of exciting artifacts, including some old parchments. These documents explain that centuries ago, as a reward for good service, Sir Francis was given Marlinspike Hall (the Bird brothers' mansion in which Tintin was kept prisoner in *The Secret of the Unicorn*) by King Charles II of England.

CAPTAIN HADDOCK'S FAMILY ESTATE

Professor Calculus buys Captain Haddock's family estate. Hergé used a French mansion—le Château de Cheverny—as the inspiration for Marlinspike Hall. The author acquired a brochure for the château, which he kept in his archives. Look at the picture of the brochure below: Hergé sketched Tintin and Captain Haddock walking up the path!

RED RACKHAM'S TREASURE!

We've found it! . . . We've found it at last: Red Rackham's treasure! . . . Look! . . . Look!

A wonderful surprise lies in store for Captain Haddock and Tintin as they explore the basement in Marlinspike Hall: it's Red Rackham's treasure. Blistering barnacles!

The Maritime Gallery

The double-adventure of *The Secret of the Unicorn* and *Red Rackham's Treasure* is finished. Captain Haddock organizes an exhibition of objects that have appeared in the adventure. But there is a last hidden detail to be discovered. Hergé thanked his friend Gérard Liger-Belair, the man who made a model of the *Unicorn*, in this drawing by putting a copy of the plan of the model (see the Young Readers Edition *The Secret of the Unicorn*) on the wall. You can just see the edge behind the figurehead of the *Unicorn*!

TINTIN'S GRAND ADVENTURE

Red Rackham's Treasure completed the first two-part story that Hergé wrote. This exciting story marked the beginning of what many people now call Hergé's "golden period," when the author wrote what would become his best-loved tales. In any case, *Red Rackham's Treasure* remains the best-selling Tintin book of all time!

Trivia: *Red Rackham's Treasure*

Hergé judged the first frame on page 25 to be one of his two favorite drawings from the Tintin books. The artist was fond of simple drawings that served their purpose!

Hergé worked 7 days a week on Red Rackham's Treasure and completed the story in 7 months.

Tintin began publication in Portuguese children's magazine Diabrete while Hergé worked on this story. But Tintin had already been published in Portuguese since 1936: it was his first foreign language!

The competition between the Paris and Greenwich Meridians for the position of Prime Meridian is part of the plot of Jules Verne's novel Twenty Thousand Leagues Under the Sea.

The original cover for *Red Rackham's Treasure* (1944)

GO ON MORE ADVENTURES WITH TINTIN!

THE SECRET OF THE UNICORN

RED RACKHAM'S TREASURE

CIGARS OF THE PHARAOH

THE BLUE LOTUS

TINTIN IN AMERICA

THE BROKEN EAR

THE BLACK ISLAND

KING OTTOKAR'S SCEPTRE

THE CRAB WITH THE GOLDEN CLAWS

THE SHOOTING STAR

ALSO AVAILABLE